S0-ARN-753

BASEBALL HALL OF FAMERS

Joe DiMaggio

Lois Sakany

the rosen publishing group's
rosen central

To my son, Isaiah

Published in 2004 by The Rosen Publishing Group, Inc.
29 East 21st Street, New York, NY 10010

Library of Congress Cataloging-in-Publication Data

Sakany, Lois.
Joe DiMaggio/by Lois Sakany.—1st ed.
  p. cm.—(Baseball Hall of Famers)
Includes bibliographical references and index.
Summary: Describes the life and career of the legendary
New York Yankees star Joe DiMaggio.
ISBN 0-8239-3779-8 (lib. bdg.)
1. DiMaggio, Joe, 1914–1999—Juvenile literature. 2.
Baseball players—United States—Biography—Juvenile
literature. [1. DiMaggio, Joe, 1914–1999. 2. Baseball players.]
I. Title. II. Series.
GV865.D5S23 2003
796.357'092—dc21
[B]

2002010756

Manufactured in the United States of America

Contents

Yankee legend Joe DiMaggio sports a winning smile in the dugout before the 1949 All-Star Game at Ebbets Field.

Introduction

Fans purposefully study and take pride in quoting their favorite player's statistics, and game announcers fill their broadcasts with observations based on how often a player hits, slugs, or steals bases. Much is made of numbers in the game of baseball. And while all good players have impressive numbers—high batting averages, plenty of runs batted in, and lots of stolen bases—the great ones have more. Joe DiMaggio, who played his entire career with the New York Yankees from 1936 to 1951, was without a doubt one of the greatest players of the game.

What made DiMaggio great? Like many of the game's best—those who will be written and talked about long after they take their last run around the bases—DiMaggio seemed born to play baseball. From the picture-perfect way in which he swung the bat to the way he gracefully strode across the outfield when chasing down fly balls, every move he made seemed almost effortless.

Even Ted Williams, one of baseball's all-time great hitters who played for the Boston Red Sox during DiMaggio's career, was forced to admit in *Joltin' Joe DiMaggio*, "In my heart, I've always felt that I was a better hitter than Joe, which [was] always my first consideration. But I have to say he was the greatest player of our time. He could do it all."

While DiMaggio may have been a natural, he never took his talents for granted. What appeared to come easy to him was due in part to his intense focus each time he walked out onto the diamond.

Just as important as his game, however, was the strength of his personality. Ever mindful of the effect of his actions on those around him, whether fans or teammates, DiMaggio never raised a fuss over a bad call. He was not a man to whom it would ever occur to complain about being a role model to children.

In fact, DiMaggio, nicknamed the Yankee Clipper, or more affectionately Joltin' Joe, was so even-tempered that when he once scuffed the ground during a game after an outfielder caught one of his center hits, the fact that he kicked up a little dirt became a newspaper story the following day.

The effect of both DiMaggio's game and his attitude toward his teammates is perhaps what truly elevates him to legendary status. It was often said that "as DiMaggio goes, so go the Yankees." In other words, DiMaggio's incredible skills combined with his solid work ethic and dignity elevated the people around him. In effect, when DiMaggio was playing well, so did the Yankees.

DiMaggio in the field during a game in a picture taken circa 1939

Streets Paved with Gold

Like many of our greatest heroes, part of what endears Joe DiMaggio to us is his humble background. With ten brothers and sisters, neither his mother nor his father pushed him to play baseball, largely because the game was unfamiliar and they were busy tending to their very large brood. Looking back, in fact, there is very little in DiMaggio's past that would predict his future as one of the game's greatest players.

Perhaps he received a good dose of determination from his father, Giuseppe DiMaggio, who was born in 1874 in Italy on Isola del Femmine, a small island located northwest of Palermo in the Golfo di Carini in Sicily. DiMaggio's mother, Rosalie Mercurio, was born on the island as well, and the two met and married there.

San Francisco's Fisherman's Wharf, pictured here, was where DiMaggio's father, a fisherman named Giuseppe, made his livelihood after his family immigrated to the United States from Sicily.

Like his father and his father's father before him, Giuseppe made his living as a fisherman. In the late 1800s, Giuseppe took a break from fishing to serve in the Italian army. Exposed to the people and places beyond the borders of his small, sleepy island, Giuseppe listened closely to the stories of riches made across the sea in America.

While others talked, Giuseppe decided to take action. Promising that he would send for her soon, he left his young wife, then pregnant with their first child, and headed to America's west coast, specifically Collinsville, located just north of San Francisco. Once there, he joined his wife's father, who had already immigrated to the small town.

Son of a Fisherman

Four years later, in 1902, he sent for Rosalie and his first daughter, who had been born not long after he left for America. The DiMaggio family grew quickly. Joe, born on November 25, 1914, was the clan's fourth son and eighth child.

Shortly after Joe was born, Giuseppe moved his family into San Francisco, where a small colony of Italian immigrants already lived. After Joe, there would be three more children, all of whom lived in the bottom apartment of a three-story building where the rent was $25 a month.

Giuseppe's boat was within walking distance, and all the children attended school in the neighborhood. At home with their parents, Italian was the language of choice, but among their friends, the children spoke English. The

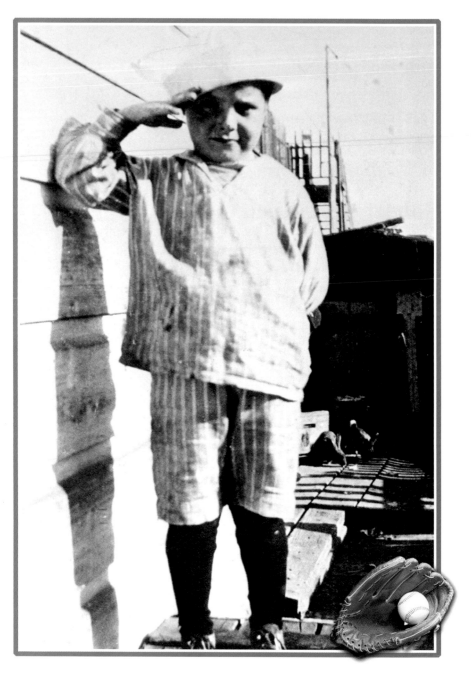

In 1917, three-year-old Joe DiMaggio salutes the cameraperson in the backyard of his family's home in Martinez, California.

family was poor, but Giuseppe worked hard so that his children never went hungry.

Even though he was perhaps more adventurous than his forefathers, Giuseppe still had an old-school mentality when it came to the future careers of his children. He expected that when his sons were old enough, they would follow him and also make their living as fishermen. Tom and Mike, the two oldest sons, did just that, but Giuseppe's next two sons, Vincent and Joe, had other ideas.

As well known as San Francisco was for its community of first-generation Italian fishermen, it was also famous as the home of the Seals, a highly successful, triple-A minor league baseball team, which was part of the Pacific Coast League. Young boys in the city were inspired by the team and played unorganized games whenever possible on empty lots and city streets. Times were tough. Most children played barehanded because they couldn't afford gloves, and rocks were often used to mark bases.

When it came time for Vincent to join his brothers and father on the boats, the young man recoiled. Giuseppe and his son fought frequently over his future in baseball, and when Vincent, who was two years older than Joe, was invited to join the Lumber League of Northern California, his father told him he couldn't go. Underage, Vincent needed his father's signature in order to join the team. Determined to play, he lied about his age, signed himself up, and ran off to play ball.

The Beginning of Great Things

Having borne the brunt of Giuseppe's anger over his decision to choose baseball as a career over fishing, Vincent, as older siblings often do, paved the way for Joe to make different career choices with less of a fight. It also helped that Joe was quieter and more obedient than his older brother Vincent.

Still, while Joe managed to avoid a future as a fisherman (he hated the smell of fish and became seasick when the water was rough), neither did he put all his time and attention on becoming a full-time baseball player.

At the time Vincent left home to play professionally, the country was in the midst of the Great Depression, and Joe decided that he should help his family. He quit school and went to work, first in a factory and later as a laborer. He played baseball only when he could find the time.

However, when the Seals signed Vincent for $150 a month, it occurred to Joe that he no longer needed to divide his attention between work and baseball. He realized it was possible to make a good living by simply doing what he loved.

In the spring of 1931, when Joe was sixteen years old, he signed up with the Jolly Nights, an organized team that played club and company teams all over the city. Just under six feet tall, he was just starting to fill out and develop the hitting strength for which he would later be world-famous. Already he was gaining a reputation on the streets of San Francisco.

By the following spring, Joe played for half a dozen different teams, running bases nearly seven days a week. Most of the time he played the position of shortstop, which, given the number of errors he was known to commit, was clearly never a position he was destined to play.

Joe was a less than perfect infielder, but he more than made up for it at bat. During one period while playing for a locally sponsored club called Sunset Produce, he was batting .632. In other words, he was knocking out a hit two out of three times he stepped up to bat. Given those numbers, it wasn't long before scouts for both the San Francisco Mission Reds and the San Francisco Seals, both semiprofessional teams, began to notice.

Once again, Joe's brother Vincent would play a part in shaping his little brother's future. Having already been recruited by the San Francisco Seals, Vincent just happened to be in on a conversation in which the team's manager, Ike Caveney, mentioned needing a stand-in shortstop for the last three games of the 1932 season. As one

DiMaggio displays his throwing arm in this picture taken on July 26, 1935, while playing outfield for the San Francisco Seals. By the following season, DiMaggio was a New York Yankee.

version of the story goes, Joe's brother didn't hesitate, "I got a brother who's a shortstop—and a good one too!"

Other accounts, which are decidedly less colorful, credit Edward "Spike" Hennessy, a scout for the Seals, for bringing Joe to the attention of the Seal's owner, Charles Graham. He had seen him hit and run and decided to sign him for the final games of the season.

Whether or not Vincent was responsible for Joe being signed to the Seals, the DiMaggio family was still close. In *Giants of Baseball*, Joe was often asked how three DiMaggio brothers (both Vince and Joe's younger brother Dom also played for major league teams) were able to play professional baseball. He explained, "If anyone wants to know why three kids in one family made it to the big leagues, they just had to know how we helped each other and how much we practiced back then."

Seal of Approval

DiMaggio played well enough in those final three games of the Seals' 1932 season to be invited to join the team the following year for spring training. As he would throughout his career, DiMaggio relied heavily on the advice of his older brother Tom when it came to negotiating contracts.

After a month of dealing, Tom was able to land a contract that paid $250 a month, twice the amount of what most rookies in the league made. At the age of seventeen, Joe was too young to sign his own contract, so his father was brought in to make it official.

As in the year before, the starting shortstop position was held by Augie Galan, a talented young infielder who would later play for the Chicago Cubs. DiMaggio got his big break when Galan was injured in the Seals' last exhibition

DiMaggio crosses home plate for the San Francisco Seals during a game in 1933, the first year he played baseball as a professional.

game. Starting at shortstop for the team's first regular season game, DiMaggio managed to commit four errors, hardly a stellar beginning.

Still, the team's manager, Ike Caveney, recognized his potential and moved him to the outfield. Even though he performed well as a fielder, he initially stumbled as a hitter. During April and May, his batting average hovered around .250 and his future with the team looked doubtful.

Then, suddenly, the dark cloud that seemed to be following his every move lifted. At the end of May, DiMaggio started hitting and the Seals started winning. By the time the team played and beat their cross-town rivals, the Missions, fans were talking about DiMaggio's hitting streak. At 30 games, he still had a ways to go before he would pass the league record set by Jack Ness, who hit in 49 straight games the year after DiMaggio was born.

62 Consecutive Games

As his streak grew and focus on DiMaggio intensified, he began to gain notoriety for his batting ability, as well as his picture-perfect stance and swing. His feet were planted wide apart, and he stood straight, with the bat cocked just behind his ear. When he swung his patented swing, he barely lifted his front foot from the dirt, and, more often than not, the result was a line drive that ripped past fielders and flew out of the park.

Soon the crowds started growing at home and away games as fans came to see whether or not this hot, new hitter would continue the streak. At the same time, press coverage heated up and reporters vied to interview the young player. Since DiMaggio was quiet and shy to the point of being introverted, it wasn't long before reporters focused on his reticent personality.

With nothing more to go on then his clipped answers, the reporters drew their own conclusions. Some writers viewed him as dull and lacking in personality, while others interpreted his lack of emotions as intense concentration. Eventually, he was tagged with the nickname "Dead Pan Joe."

Still, the streak continued. Prior to the game that would break the previous record held by Ness, a ceremony was given in San Francisco, at which DiMaggio was presented with gifts and a bonus check from the Seals. At game 62, DiMaggio's streak ended. He was just eighteen years old. To this day, his record still stands in the Pacific Coast League.

At the season's end, DiMaggio's statistics were impressive: a .340 batting average, 259 hits in 187 games, 28 home runs, 45 doubles, 13 triples, 169 RBIs, and 129 runs scored. Locals were no longer alone in their admiration.

Getting an early start at practice, DiMaggio is airborne, catching fly balls in his first picture in a Yankee uniform. DiMaggio was the first to show up at training camp in St. Petersburg, Florida.

By the end of the 1933 season, all sixteen major league teams had sent scouts to check out the game's newest and brightest phenomenon.

The New York Yankees

The New York Yankees were especially keen on picking up DiMaggio. Babe Ruth was on the verge of retiring, and, worse yet, the Yankees hadn't won a pennant that year. Even though Lou Gehrig was playing well, it was clear that he alone couldn't lead the team to a championship.

At the time DiMaggio was playing ball, minor league teams existed independently from the major leagues. Teams such as the Seals would scout out local talent, and, if a player bloomed, his contract would be sold to a major league team.

At the end of DiMaggio's amazing season, his price tag, as set by the Seals' owner, Charles Graham, was $75,000. As talented as he may have been, the country was still in the midst of the Great Depression, and no major league team was willing to gamble that kind of money on a rookie.

The Yankees' hesitation proved wise when, at the start of the 1934 season, DiMaggio injured his knee while getting off a bus. He was out of the lineup for the next six weeks and struggled with the injury for the rest of the season. Despite the setback, which resulted in DiMaggio missing more than 70 games, he still ended up with a .341 batting average.

The Yankees remained interested in DiMaggio, though because of his knee damage, they were no longer willing to pay his pre-injury price of $75,000. Hard bargaining followed, and eventually, the Yankees' general manager, Ed Barrow, agreed to a price of $25,000 plus five players.

As part of the agreement, DiMaggio would play one more year with the Seals. If the rising outfielder made it through the season without recurring knee problems, the Seals would get their money and DiMaggio would become a major leaguer.

The 1935 season was an incredible year for DiMaggio. He was managed that year by Francis

On July 14, 1933, Mayor Angelo Rossi of San Francisco presents a gift watch to DiMaggio for his record-breaking stint playing for the Seals in the Pacific Coast League.

Joseph "Lefty" O'Doul. Once one of the game's great hitters, O'Doul had played in Yankee Stadium and imparted all the wisdom he could upon DiMaggio about playing in the majors.

Under O'Doul's guidance, DiMaggio raised his batting average to .398 and led his team to win the Pacific Coast League pennant. To top it off, he was also voted the league's MVP. Now he could rest assured that he would start the following season with the New York Yankees.

The Rookie

The following spring, DiMaggio headed across the country by car, accompanied by established Yankee players and fellow San Franciscans Tony Lazzeri and Frank Crosetti. They were headed to the Yankees' spring training camp in St. Petersburg, Florida. Neither Lazzeri nor Crosetti were much more talkative than DiMaggio, and it is said that the three drove in silence for most of the trip.

When DiMaggio was told it was his turn to take the wheel, he barely mumbled back that he didn't know how to drive. Without missing a step, Crosetti jokingly replied, "Let's throw the bum out!" While DiMaggio managed to hold on to his place in the car, little more was said.

All that silence, however, was more than made up for by the reporters awaiting his arrival

DiMaggio *(right)* takes a breather with Yankee teammates Frank Crosetti *(left)* and Tony Lazzeri *(center)* during a game on September 1, 1936. All three men were from San Francisco.

at camp. As big league veterans based in media-crazed New York, Lazzeri and Crosetti knew what was coming and aimed for an evening arrival to avoid the onslaught. It didn't make much of a difference. The hullabaloo started promptly the next morning and signaled the end of DiMaggio's life as just another ballplayer. Fame was upon him. It was a status with which he would never feel entirely comfortable.

On March 1, 1936, DiMaggio showed up for his first team workout with the New York Yankees. Half a dozen or more sportswriters were there as well, ready to analyze and report on number 18's every move.

DiMaggio didn't disappoint. At his first batting practice, he smashed three balls clean over the left field fence. At practice after practice, DiMaggio continued to delight, and soon it was clear that his story was one with legs. Rather than murmur among themselves over his potential, reporters began to loudly shout it. One sportswriter, Dan Daniel, writing for the *World-Telegram*, proclaimed about DiMaggio: "Here is the replacement for Babe Ruth."

In his first exhibition game, played against the St. Louis Cardinals, manager Joe McCarthy placed the young player third in the lineup (not coincidentally, Babe Ruth's old spot). In his first time at bat, he smacked out a triple and followed with three more singles.

Word of his talents spread quickly, and by his third game, the crowds were already

From the very beginning and throughout his career, DiMaggio was known for his sheer hitting power and superb fielding abilities.

growing. His average was well over .500 when, in a game against the Cincinnati Reds, his meteoric rise was temporarily halted.

Beset by Injury

Sliding into second on a force play, the second baseman stepped on DiMaggio's foot. The next day, it was so bruised and swollen that he was unable to play. The trainer, "Doc" Painter, recommended heat therapy and placed DiMaggio's foot into a machine that would warm it.

Left alone, he said nothing as the heat on his foot slowly increased. Eventually, the rising temperature became painful, but DiMaggio still said nothing. It didn't occur to him to complain or to question the trainer's expertise. Stoically obeying, he withstood the excruciating pain of a machine that burned his foot so badly that he would miss more than a month of games—the last of spring exhibition and the first three weeks of the season.

DiMaggio made his major league debut on a Sunday in May, sporting the more prestigious number 9 (which would soon be changed to number 5) and played to a packed stadium. Starting in left field, he thrilled the crowd with two singles and a triple. When he returned from his injury, the Yankees were in second place to the Boston Red Sox. Within a week, the team had moved ahead of Boston into the first place position.

More Than Just a Hitter

Though DiMaggio was first noted for his superb hitting, fans of the game quickly noticed that he did not only hit well, he did everything well. Just as he was off the field, DiMaggio was quietly dignified while playing baseball. Combining a sharp eye with an ability to accelerate quickly from a standing position (not to mention great instincts), DiMaggio never seemed to sweat while chasing hits to the outfield. Instead, observers frequently mentioned how effortless his stride was, and how, no matter how far the ball was hit, he always seemed to be in the right place at the right time.

His arm was also strong and his aim dead-on. In his first year of baseball, fans didn't have to wait long to see the power of his throw. Early in the season, in a game against Detroit, the opposing team had runners on first and third. There were no outs and the score was tied.

A pop fly was hit into far left field. Peter Fox, who was on third base and was one of the fastest runners in the league, leaned forward, ready to race home as soon as he got the go-ahead from the third base coach. He never got there. A good five feet from the plate, he was tagged out by the catcher, the recipient of a laser-quick throw from the rookie in left field.

To top off his all-around game, DiMaggio was an excellent base runner. Though by no means the fastest in the majors, he was nevertheless the shrewdest. His sharp sight in all likelihood included excellent peripheral vision, a gift that enabled him to take in a greater range of action.

Interest in DiMaggio wasn't limited only to New York fans, either, and as the season progressed, various onlookers witnessed the already storied rookie. When it came to vote for an all-star outfielder, he won not just by the strength of New York fans but of admirers from coast to coast.

After his performance in that year's All-Star Game, it's a good bet that DiMaggio, for a minute, wished he wasn't quite so popular. In one of the lower moments of his first year in the majors, he came up to bat four times and each time walked away empty handed. In the seventh inning, he left the bases loaded, and in the ninth, he left the tying run on second base.

Worse yet, his poor fielding in the fifth led to an unearned run that would eventually lose the game for the National League.

With the memory of the failed All-Star Game just weeks behind him, DiMaggio would stumble again, this time literally. Positioned in right field, he took off like a shot for a hit heading quickly to right center field. Intensely focused on reaching the ball before it dropped to the ground, DiMaggio failed to notice that the center fielder, Myril Hoag, was also chasing the ball. The two players collided head-on and fell to the ground.

Two days after the incident, Hoag was admitted to the hospital because of complications resulting from the collision. DiMaggio, with only a headache, was moved to center field. He would reign supreme in this position for the rest of his days. Had Hoag's career ended with that fateful collision, then perhaps DiMaggio would have lost a bit of his luster. Fortunately, Hoag recovered completely and continued to play in the big leagues for nearly another decade.

Cruising to Victory

Midseason mishaps aside, DiMaggio spent the second half leading the Yankees to victory, clinching the pennant on September 9, the earliest date in the history of major league baseball. DiMaggio ended the season with impressive numbers: a .323 batting average, 49 home runs, and 152 RBIs. However, the winning wasn't over yet.

In the fall of 1936, the World Series featured the New York Yankees versus the New York Giants. The match was dubbed the Subway Series, though in reality, there was no need to take a subway from one stadium to the other. The Polo Grounds, where the Giants played, and Yankee Stadium were both located in the Bronx, and the two stadiums were a fifteen-minute-walk away from each other.

As with any series in which the opposing teams share the same city, the advent of the 1936 World Series was endlessly analyzed in the press. Certainly, there was enough hype that President Franklin D. Roosevelt, who was in the midst of a reelection campaign, not

Yankee pitcher Bump Hadley and third baseman Red Rolfe film movies of their star rookie DiMaggio during practice at Yankee Stadium before the 1936 World Series.

only attended Game 2 but stayed through to the end of the game.

The Yankees were soundly defeated in Game 1, 6–1, but from that point on, despite one more win from the Giants, the team dominated the series and eventually won four games to two. DiMaggio's contribution came in the form of a .347 batting average. The Giants' manager, Bill Terry, commented on DiMaggio's performance following the series in the book *I Remember Joe DiMaggio:* "I've always heard that one player could make the difference between a losing team and a winner, and I never believed it. Now I know it's true."

Family Matters

After such a brilliant rookie year, Joe DiMaggio surely could have spent his off-season living it up in New York City. Given his loyalty to those he loved, however, the idea of doing anything other than heading straight back to San Francisco was probably never even a consideration.

For the regular season of his rookie year, DiMaggio had been paid a salary of $8,500 and an additional bonus of $6,400 for winning the World Series. Just under $15,000 for a year of playing baseball may not seem like much money today, but back then it was the salary of a rich man. Later, DiMaggio would be criticized for being both frugal and obsessed with money. However, it wasn't borne out by his actions. When he returned home, he used his salary to buy his older brother Mike another boat to add to his fleet and made plans to invest in a

Joe and his brother Dominic DiMaggio sit down for a home-cooked meal prepared by their mother, Rosalie DiMaggio, on October 24, 1947.

restaurant that his brother Tom planned to build on Fisherman's Wharf in San Francisco.

Never forgetting how hard both his mother and father had worked to provide for their family, DiMaggio bought them a new home, moving them from the cramped apartment in which he grew up to a roomy house in the Marina District of San Francisco.

When it came to financial matters, DiMaggio once again turned to his family for advice. In the early part of his career, he turned to his older brother Tom to help him negotiate his yearly contract.

A Hard Bargainer

His agreement wasn't much of an issue for the 1937 season. When Yankee general manager Ed Barrow offered him the same salary from the year before, he turned it down without a thought. When a second contract was sent to him for $15,000, DiMaggio let it be known that he wanted $20,000.

By the time spring training began, everyone was there except DiMaggio and his two teammates, first baseman Lou Gehrig and pitcher Red Ruffing. Realizing how far down he was on the totem pole as a second-year player, DiMaggio buckled first and, depending on the source, settled for either a salary of $15,000 or $17,500.

DiMaggio was well worth the higher figure. As in the previous year, he got off to a late start, but he ended the season with a .346 batting average, 35 doubles, 15 triples, 46 home runs, and 167 runs batted in. When the season was finished, he didn't win the MVP award, but he came in a close second, narrowly missing by just four votes.

In the postseason, the Yankees once again went head-to-head with the Giants. They put them down 4–1 with even more ease than the year before, with DiMaggio batting 6 for 22 with one home run, two runs scored, and four runs batted in.

When he headed back home at the end of the series, he did so with the firm belief that he had proven his worth. After all, he was no longer the new kid on the block. Whatever doubts that management might have had about his ability to perform consistently had to have been eased by his winning performance.

Though it is certain that he consulted frequently with his brother Tom regarding negotiations, he didn't need anyone to tell him to ignore the proposal the organization mailed him in 1938. In it, the Yankees promised to pay the rising star the exact same amount that he had been paid the year before.

Concluding that a face-to-face meeting would be a more advantageous forum in which

DiMaggio gets his second home run in the first game of a doubleheader against the Philadelphia Athletics on June 28, 1939. The Yankees broke all home run records during this series, in which they hit 13 homers in a two-day period.

to negotiate a higher salary, he headed to New York to meet with Barrow and Col. Jacob Ruppert, who owned the Yankees.

As agreed, he arrived at the meeting at 10:30 AM, but he was made to wait 45 minutes outside his bosses' door. The owners offered him $25,000—an offer that DiMaggio flatly refused. He left the office empty-handed and angry, and, as instructed by Barrow and Ruppert, made no statement to the press regarding the meeting.

When spring training began, DiMaggio was still in San Francisco where he kept busy helping his brother Tom with the family's new restaurant. To keep in shape, he occasionally worked out with the San Francisco Seals.

The Fans Turn

Pressure mounted in mid-March when Gehrig accepted a $3,000 raise and signed a contract for $39,000. Meanwhile, Ruppert, growing impatient, added to the pressure by making statements to the press about the young player's selfishness. In what seemed like a quick and dramatic turn, the once adoring press turned on DiMaggio and slammed him as a money-grubber and an ingrate. When spring training began and ended without DiMaggio, his once ardent fans began to grumble, too.

The sad reality was that the Yankees could not only afford DiMaggio's salary demand, they probably knew he was worth at least that much. At the time, (and for many years after), players had little to no negotiating power.

Batting for more money was not an option. If a player didn't like the terms being offered by his team, there was little he could do other than hope for the best. As a result, while Barrow and Ruppert may have been impressed by DiMaggio's talents, they were more infuriated by his attempt to change the status quo, and they were determined to put him in his place.

On opening day, the team played Boston without DiMaggio and lost. When word got back to him that both his manager and his teammates were starting to make disparaging comments, he finally gave in. The fact that DiMaggio finally agreed to their terms wasn't enough for the owners. Adding insult to injury, the Yankees docked his salary for each game he missed and then declared that he would also forego pay for the upcoming games in which he couldn't play because he was getting back in shape.

It was a humiliating experience for the proud DiMaggio. Even after he returned and began performing true to form once again, crowds booed him and the press criticized him. And while he never let the Yankees' tough stance compromise his play, from that point forward, his view on the game was considerably less lighthearted.

When the 1938 season ended, the Yankees sat firmly in first place. In the World Series, the Chicago Cubs were eliminated and the Yanks were crowned champions after sweeping the series 4–0.

The following year, DiMaggio signed his contract without fanfare. It was a significant year. Just before the start of the season, Colonel Jacob Ruppert, the hard-nosed owner of the Yankees, died at seventy-two years of age, and early in May, Gehrig, longtime Yankee first

New York mayor Fiorello H. LaGuardia honors DiMaggio with a watch and citation just before a game with the Cleveland Indians on August 23, 1940. DiMaggio had just been named the American League's Most Valuable Player for 1939.

baseman and one of the team's greatest players, took himself out of the lineup for the first time in 2,130 games. Though he didn't know it at the time, he was suffering from a fatal illness that would soon take his life.

The season ended on a high note for DiMaggio. After the Yankees won their third consecutive World Series, DiMaggio, who batted .380 for the season, was awarded his first MVP award.

Joe and his wife Dorothy Arnold share a smile as DiMaggio holds up a baseball with the magic number 45 on it. DiMaggio had a 45-game consecutive hitting streak when this picture was taken on July 2, 1941.

When he returned home to San Francisco that fall, Dorothy Arnold, an actress he had been dating for two years, accompanied him. On November 19, the two were married in the same Catholic church that DiMaggio had attended as a youth. The crush of people outside the church who were vying to get a view of the couple was so huge that Joe's two brothers Vincent and Tom barely saw the ceremony.

The convergence of his private and public life was a theme that DiMaggio would struggle with for years. Though resigned to, and even accepting of, his role as a baseball hero, the intensely private ballplayer fought hard to keep himself and those he loved out of the limelight. His struggle for privacy became one of the few things in life at which DiMaggio was unsuccessful.

The Streak

Although it is often said that records are made to be broken, DiMaggio's 1941 record of safely hitting in 56 consecutive games is one that may survive for the ages. Thirty-seven years after DiMaggio set the record, Pete Rose neared it with 44 straight games, but since then, no other player has come closer.

In 1941, hopes for a good season were not particularly high among Yankee fans. The previous year, the team had ended the season stuck in third place, and little more than two months into the season, the Yanks were playing well below .500.

DiMaggio's streak started on May 15 during a game against the Chicago White Sox. He batted a single to left field that brought home Yankee shortstop Phil Rizzuto. It didn't matter. The Yankees lost yet another game, and fans were beginning to wonder just how great their center fielder really was.

The Yankees were on the road when the team received the sad news that their team captain, Lou Gehrig, had died. Well known for his own ability to streak, prior to succumbing to illness, the thirty-seven-year-old Gehrig—aptly nicknamed the Iron Horse—had played 2,130 games without missing one.

Even though the Yankees lost to the Detroit Tigers the following day, DiMaggio led off the fourth inning with a home run and maintained his streak.

At 20 games, the press had not yet taken notice of DiMaggio's streak. In fact, if anyone was receiving attention for his prowess at bat, it was Ted Williams, who had hit safely in 22 games and was batting .434. However, when Williams's luck ended at 23 games, the fans and the press began to focus instead on DiMaggio.

Challenges Along the Way

Though there were a handful of close calls along the way, one of DiMaggio's biggest challenges came in the fortieth game in his streak against the Philadelphia Athletics' pitcher Johnny Babich, who knew DiMaggio from the Pacific Coast League. Frequently successful at shutting down the Yankees, Babich was determined to end DiMaggio's hitting streak.

He vowed to pitch only junk so that even if DiMaggio walked every time he came to bat, at least he wouldn't get a hit under Babich's watch. When DiMaggio stepped up to the plate for the first time that day, as predicted, Babich threw four bad pitches. In his second at bat with the count at three balls and no strikes, DiMaggio looked over at the third-base coach, who, under any other circumstances, would have instructed him to take the next pitch. Knowing Babich's promise, the third-base coach gave him the go-ahead to hit. Sure enough, the next pitch was pure junk, but DiMaggio still managed to reach out and whacked it into center field for a double.

After game 41, which was the first of a doubleheader, DiMaggio discovered that his bat had been stolen from the dugout by a fan. The bat was a 36-inch, 36-ounce Louisville Slugger, and

DiMaggio was crushed to discover it gone. After going hitless his first three times at bat, teammate Tommy Henrich convinced him to use his bat, which DiMaggio had given to him earlier in the season. In the seventh inning, he knocked a single into left field and extended his streak to 42 games.

On July 2, DiMaggio broke the league record set in 1897 by Willie Keeler, who had safely hit in 44 consecutive games. His lone shot in that game against the Boston Red Sox came in the seventh inning. Fittingly enough, it was a home run.

Shortly after the record was broken, an anonymous caller telephoned the Yankee clubhouse and let it be known that he knew the location of DiMaggio's stolen bat. Through an intermediary, the bat was returned, and in his next two games—a double header against the Philadelphia Athletics—he hit three singles, two doubles, and a triple, which was more than he needed to put his streak at 48.

By this time, talk of DiMaggio's streak was a daily topic of conversation among baseball fans and even among those less interested in the sport. Radio broadcasts interrupted programs to report on his day-to-day progress and "Joltin' Joe DiMaggio" was a popular song on jukeboxes all over the country.

In Boston, during Red Sox games at Fenway Park, the scorekeeper would pass information about DiMaggio's streak to left fielder Ted Williams, who would in turn call over to Joe's brother Dom, playing in center field.

As amazing as DiMaggio's streak was, the national obsession with it was probably due in part to its lightheartedness as a news item. At the time, it was a welcome distraction from the news coming from Europe, where German troops were rolling across the countryside and World War II was raging.

The Streak Ends

Two months after it began, DiMaggio's streak ended at 56 games on July 17 in Cleveland. The Yankees faced the Indians that night in front of a crowd of 67,468 fans—the largest audience ever to see a night game in the major leagues. DiMaggio grounded out in his first at bat and was walked in his second at bat. In response, the crowd, which

Manager Joe McCarthy puts his arm around DiMaggio after the Yankees beat the Cleveland Indians 4–3 on July 17, 1941, in Cleveland, Ohio.

was surely as big as it was because everyone had come to see DiMaggio hit, booed their own pitcher.

Two more times he came to bat and two more times he grounded out. He remarked on the game in *DiMaggio, The Last American Knight* and said, "I'm glad it's over."

And while the ending of the streak may have saddened baseball fans across the country, the teams that actually had to compete against the Yankees were probably relieved. During DiMaggio's streak, the Yankees won 41 games

Adoring parents Joe and Dorothy enjoy Christmas Eve with three-month-old Joe DiMaggio Jr. at their West End Avenue home in 1941.

and lost only 13 with two ties. More important, though they were in fourth place when the streak started, they were in first when it ended.

DiMaggio's own statistics during the streak were impressive. He had a .408 batting average and a total of 91 hits, including 16 doubles, four triples, and 15 home runs. And during 223 at bats, he struck out only seven times. After the streak ended, he immediately started another one and hit safely in 16 more games. During the 1941 season, he hit safely in 72 out of 73 games.

When it ended, the Yankees finished in first place, 17 games ahead of their rivals, the Boston Red Sox. DiMaggio was voted the league's MVP, beating out Williams, who had finished the season with .406. The Yanks then went on to beat cross-town rivals the Brooklyn Dodgers four games to one in the World Series.

To top it all off, just after the World Series ended, DiMaggio's wife, Dorothy, gave birth to his son, Joe Jr., on October 23. DiMaggio couldn't have been more thrilled. Not only did he have a banner year, he was now the proud father of a healthy baby boy.

The Lost Years

With as much good fortune as was bestowed on him in 1941, perhaps the fates concluded that DiMaggio's luck would eventually run cool.

As he had before, the now-famous ballplayer spent the first part of spring training holding out for a higher salary. Unlike prior seasons, however, when DiMaggio returned to play, he found himself struggling. By the end of June, he was batting just .268.

Still, he redeemed himself in the months to follow, and the Yankees managed to finish the season in first place anyway. Odds-makers favored the Yanks in the 1942 World Series, but after the St. Louis Cardinals rallied in the ninth inning of Game 1 to win, the Yankees never got back on track. Though DiMaggio batted well, the Yankees lost that series four games to one.

The news got worse for DiMaggio when in December his wife of just three years filed papers for divorce. It was far from a shocking announcement. Dorothy, a former actress, never adjusted to life as a housewife, and DiMaggio couldn't be the patriarch that his father was. Fame pushed and pulled him in different directions, and he was ultimately too distracted to be either a good husband or father.

Nonetheless, DiMaggio couldn't bear the idea of a breakup, so he worked to convince her to reconcile. Though she relented, it wouldn't last. Eight months later, Dorothy filed for divorce again. And while DiMaggio could no longer convince her to change her mind, the two continued to have an on-and-off romance for years.

Uncle Sam Wants You

News of the their reconciliation was shortly followed by the announcement that DiMaggio would not be joining the Yankees for the spring of 1943. The country was in the midst of World War II, and DiMaggio would instead be joining the U.S. Air Army Corps.

DiMaggio is pictured here with fellow baseball player turned air force recruit Harold "Pee Wee" Reese *(second from right)*. The two men in military uniforms, from right to left, are Vice Admiral Robert L. Ghormley and Brigadier General William J. Flood. DiMaggio reached the level of sergeant during his stint in the air force.

He enlisted in San Francisco in January and one month later reported to the army reception center at Santa Ana Army Airfield Base in Santa Ana, California. He may have been an enlisted man, but while he served, the only weapon he used with any regularity was a baseball bat.

He played with the air force team briefly in Santa Ana before he was shipped to Hawaii, where he played center field for the Seventh Air Force team. DiMaggio wasn't the only major leaguer to join the military. His team included several other well-known players, and when they played a game against a navy team in June, 20,000 fans attended.

While life in the military may have seemed easy, the divorce coupled with the uncertainty of his career stressed DiMaggio, and by the end of that summer it began to affect his health. He was hospitalized in Hawaii with ulcers, which were hardly helped by his refusal to quit smoking and temper his heavy coffee-drinking habit.

Meanwhile, the baseball season continued. In the fall of 1943, the Yankees went to the World Series again. They played the St. Louis Cardinals this time and beat them four games to two. They won it again the following year against the St. Louis Browns.

It's likely that DiMaggio's heavy thoughts were lifted when he was transferred by the air force to the Redistribution Center in Atlantic City, New Jersey. Surely it wasn't just a coincidence that the Yankees were also in Atlantic

City training and preparing for the 1944 season. Once again, DiMaggio the soldier found himself spending more time in batting practice than in target practice.

Service Takes Its Toll

DiMaggio's ulcers continued to flare up, and in August, he was sent to a hospital in St. Petersburg, Florida, to recuperate. While he was in the military, Ruppert's heirs sold the Yankees for $2.8 million. The buyers were Dan Topping, Del Webb, and Larry MacPhail, who was also the new team president. MacPhail called DiMaggio while he was convalescing in Florida and let him know that the Yankees were very interested in re-signing their star player.

On September 14, 1945, DiMaggio was granted a medical discharge, and he immediately headed back to New York City. San Francisco was no longer the place he called home.

Life was starting to improve for DiMaggio. He, his son, and his former wife, Dorothy, were together again in New York, and in collaboration with sportswriter Tom Meany, he was working on

Two of the new owners of the Yankees, Larry MacPhail *(left)* and Del Webb, watch the opening game of the International League, between Newark and Toronto, on April 10, 1945.

a book entitled *Lucky to Be a Yankee*. For DiMaggio, both events were signs that his life might actually be going back to normal.

Best of all, in November he met with the new Yankee owner and formally signed for the 1946 season. In a break from his past squabbles with management over the terms of his contract, this time the negotiations were smooth, a nice beginning for a comeback.

Return to Glory

Three years away from playing professional baseball did not sit well with DiMaggio. The ease with which he negotiated his contract meant that he was able to start spring training on the first day, but the unusually early start didn't seem to help his performance much. Compounding the problem was his age. At 31, he was still a young man, but he was not able to bounce back from injuries and illnesses as quickly as he did when he was in his twenties.

DiMaggio was suffering from a bad cold when the Yankees met the St. Louis Browns in May. Perhaps as a younger man, a minor illness might not have affected his play, but on that day, he committed two horrendous fielding errors. With the Yankees deep in second place, the fans, not interested in patiently awaiting the return of the player they remembered, booed him loudly.

In May 1949, DiMaggio returned to the Yankees' lineup after 41 days spent treating an injured heel. Illnesses and injuries troubled DiMaggio a great deal in his later career.

Worse yet, manager Joe McCarthy, whom DiMaggio admired, was clashing with the team's new ownership and resigned early in the season. Yankee catcher Bill Dickey took over as manager, and while he was popular with the players, DiMaggio and the Yankees continued to struggle. Before the end of the season, Dickey was gone, too, replaced by Johnny Neun, who would remain only to the season's end.

By early July, while sliding into second base, DiMaggio suffered the first in a series of injuries that would nag at his ability to perform for the remainder of his career. Not only would he be out of the lineup until August, he was also unable to play in the All-Star Game for the first time.

DiMaggio finished the season with a .290 batting average. His other numbers were also respectable, and the Yankees finished in third place, though for the Yankees anything short of a championship was considered an utter failure. Though it never materialized, the team's owners were disappointed enough with his performance to circulate rumors of a trade.

Injuries Take Their Toll

With his hopes set high on redeeming himself in the 1947 season, nagging pain derailed DiMaggio's aspiration for a grand comeback. In January, he was forced to undergo an operation to remove a bone spur from his left heel, and once again he missed spring training. The injury took longer than expected to heal, and DiMaggio wasn't back in the lineup until late in May.

The Yanks were in fourth place when he rejoined the team, and DiMaggio's bat began to heat up and the team began their ascension toward first place. From mid-June to mid-July, they recorded 19 straight victories and from that point on dominated the American League with ease.

Just across the river, in the National League, the Brooklyn Dodgers were also throttling the competition. As DiMaggio did in his first year with the Yankees, rookie Jackie Robinson, the first African American man to play in the major leagues, led the Dodgers.

The World Series between the rival teams was intense. When the Yankees took the first two games of the series at Yankee Stadium, fans were certain that the series was over. But the Dodgers fought back, and by the end of Game 4, each team had won two games. The series dragged on to Game 7, but the Yankees prevailed, winning the final contest, 3–1.

That winter, DiMaggio had yet another operation, this one on the elbow of his throwing arm, an injury that was as scary as any he had

The 1947 World Series pitted the Yankees against the newest rising star of baseball, the Brooklyn Dodgers' Jackie Robinson, the first African American to play in the major leagues. The Yankees finally won the series when they beat the Dodgers in Game 7.

experienced. A big part of his reputation was based on the speed and accuracy of that arm. Even though he joked with the press in the hospital and made light of his new cast, DiMaggio never liked hospitals. He left abruptly one night, never bothering to return, much less officially check out.

The Yankees started with a new manager, Bucky Harris, and high hopes for another season in which they would cruise easily to a first place finish. But it would not be—the team instead battled with the Boston Red Sox and the Cleveland Indians for the top spot all season long.

Meanwhile, DiMaggio was waging his own private war with nagging foot and leg injuries. Although he did his best to play through the pain, by mid-summer it was clear that his pain was affecting his ability to effectively patrol the outfield. Joe Trimble, a well-known reporter for the *Daily News*, suggested that perhaps the ball-player should make the switch to first base, where the ability to run quickly was less of an issue.

Fans began to wonder if the great Yankee dynasty as led by DiMaggio was beginning to crumble. Further disheartening fans and players alike, Babe Ruth, one of the Yankees' most beloved players, succumbed to cancer that August.

In September, the Boston Red Sox, the Cleveland Indians, and the New York Yankees were in a tight race for first place with the winner advancing to the World Series. The Yankees were eliminated from the race in the end, but in their final game against Boston in Fenway Park, DiMaggio—despite excruciating pain—insisted on playing. If Boston, whose center fielder was none other than his brother Dom, was going to win the pennant, they were going to have to go through DiMaggio to get it.

DiMaggio went to bat five times and had four hits. His final time at bat, he hit a single and clearly had difficulty running to first base. Despite all his efforts, however, Boston was ahead at that point by five, and the game was clearly out of the Yankees' reach.

Harris sent in a pinch runner for the center fielder, and DiMaggio limped to the dugout. Despite the intense rivalry that existed between the two teams, so touched were fans by his bravery that they rose to their feet and gave one of their most hated rivals a rousing ovation.

The Final Years

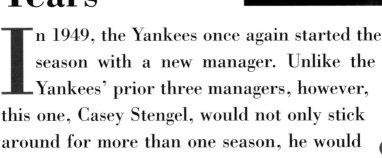

In 1949, the Yankees once again started the season with a new manager. Unlike the Yankees' prior three managers, however, this one, Casey Stengel, would not only stick around for more than one season, he would herald in a new era of winning for the team.

Once again, painful injuries kept Joe DiMaggio out of the lineup that spring. However, it was his heart that hurt when he got word from his family that his father had died in May, just one month after he had passed the U.S. test for naturalization.

DiMaggio rejoined the team in June and helped to put the Yankees back into first place by midseason. By the time October rolled around, they were tied with the Red Sox. The entire season would come down to a two-game series pitting the Yankees at home against the Red Sox.

Yankee manager Casey Stengel looks on as DiMaggio gets his heel examined during a visit to a hospital in St. Petersburg, Florida, on March 5, 1949.

A week prior to the series, DiMaggio became ill with a virus and was forced to sit out a week's worth of games. On October 1, the Yankees were scheduled to play the first of their final two games. The day had also been designated "Joe DiMaggio Day," a fan appreciation day on which DiMaggio would be presented with $50,000 worth of gifts.

Still weak and a good 15 pounds lighter from illness, DiMaggio was determined to play. Prior to the game, he spoke to the crowd and made a speech, which he finished with the now famous statement, "I want to thank the good Lord for making me a Yankee."

In the two-game series, the Yankees won Game 1 and were winning 1–0 until the bottom of the eighth inning in Game 2. They scored four more runs in that inning, but the Red Sox answered with three in the top of the ninth. After chasing down the triple that scored two of those runs, DiMaggio, crippled by foot pain, called a time-out and asked to be removed from the game.

The Yankees held on to the victory and met the Brooklyn Dodgers in the World Series. They won the series 4–1, and, later that year, the

Associated Press voted DiMaggio the greatest comeback for 1949, beating the Yankee team as a whole by one vote.

Financial Recognition

Near the end of his career, DiMaggio finally received the salary he felt he had long deserved. He signed a contract for the 1950 season that would pay him $100,000, making him the highest paid player in the league. At the time of the signing, he told the press that he hoped to win at least two more championships before retiring.

In June, after a rocky spring, DiMaggio hit his 2,000th hit in an 8–2 victory over the Cleveland Indians. His injuries, however, continued to compromise his play, and by mid-July, Stengel moved him to first base. DiMaggio made the move without complaint and performed well, but he was not happy there and soon returned to his spot in center field.

In August, he experienced a terrible batting slump, connecting for just 4 hits in 38 times at bat. Now, not only was his fielding suffering, so was his

Johnny Mize crosses home for the 324th time and is congratulated by DiMaggio, who still leads him with 334, during a July 21, 1950, game against the Detroit Tigers.

hitting, and Stengel made the difficult decision to bench one of the game's all-time greats.

Time was running out for DiMaggio, and no one knew it better than he did. Still, his pride wouldn't let him give up without a fight, and in September, he redeemed himself by batting well over .300 and hitting safely in 19 straight games.

In the fall, the Yankees once again made it to the World Series, where they played against the Philadelphia Athletics. During the championship, DiMaggio had the team's highest batting average, and during Game 2, he hit a home run that won the game. DiMaggio may not have been the same player he was as a young man, but he still had enough left to lead his team to victory in a World Series in which the Athletics were swept in four games.

The Final Year

DiMaggio's last year in the majors was the 1951 season. He planned to wait until the season was over to make an official announcement, but the rumors began to circulate with the start of spring training. That same pride that had enabled him to persevere through agonizing injuries wouldn't let him continue to play if his performance was anything less than exceptional.

Meanwhile, just as he had entered the game in time to fill Babe Ruth's enormous shoes, a nineteen-year-old from Oklahoma was making a name for himself at the Yankees' rookie camp. His name was Mickey Mantle, and even DiMaggio, whose standards were very high, commented that the young Mantle was the greatest rookie he'd ever seen. The torch was ready to be passed.

DiMaggio, however, wasn't quite through yet. Playing with injuries, once again he had a poor spring. Worse yet, his mother, who had been diagnosed with cancer in June, slipped into a coma, and though DiMaggio took the first flight home, she died shortly after his arrival.

All season long, DiMaggio's batting average hovered around .250. On September 16, the Yankees were to start a two-game series against the Cleveland Indians. The New York team was one game behind the Indians and anything other than two wins would put them in second place.

Then it finally happened. Mantle (who had been called up again from the Yankees' farm team) got to first on a bunt. Future Hall-of-Famer and Yankee catcher Yogi Berra stepped up to bat, and the pitcher intentionally walked him in order to pitch to DiMaggio, who was on deck.

Baseball Hall of Fame official R. D. Spraker flanks DiMaggio, who is turning over his jersey to the National Baseball Hall of Fame. The Yankees officially retired DiMaggio's number on April 18, 1952.

The fans couldn't believe what they were seeing and immediately began booing. No matter what his batting average may have been, no one had the right to disrespect DiMaggio, who was also furious. The count was 1-2 when he exacted his revenge on the pitcher by driving a triple to the wall, driving in two runs. The crowd roared, and the game ended with the Yanks ahead 5–1 and tied for first place. From that point on, the Indians dropped out of contention.

That year, the Yankees beat out Boston for the pennant and in another subway series beat the New York Giants in six games. In his lucky 13 years with the Yankees, DiMaggio had won 10 pennants and 9 World Series titles. It was no wonder that Yankee ownership did their best to convince DiMaggio to stay on. They even offered to pay him the same salary, though he would not be expected to play in every game. DiMaggio wouldn't have it. He wanted to retire on a high note. In December, according to *Joe DiMaggio: An Informal Biography*, he met with the press and made the official announcement: "I've played my last game of ball."

Marilyn Monroe

W hile Joe DiMaggio may have been saddened to leave the game behind, he had to have been relieved to say good-bye to the daily scrutiny from fans and the media. Fame, however, was not yet through with DiMaggio.

As do many men, DiMaggio had an eye for pretty women. Perhaps, in a true case of opposites attracting, the reserved, if not downright shy, DiMaggio also had a penchant for women who were not just easy on the eyes but also spirited—case in point, his ex-wife Dorothy Arnold. Though the two had long since separated, when they would meet ostensibly because of Joe Jr., he still enjoyed her upbeat personality, and even up until he announced his retirement, tossed around the possibility of reconciling with her again.

Those on-again-off-again plans were finally put to rest forever in the spring following his retirement. While visiting Los Angeles to participate in a charity baseball game, he was reading the local newspaper and came across a photo of a young starlet who not only possessed dazzling good looks but eyes that beamed mischief. He was immediately smitten and determined to meet the up-and-coming star who was none other than Marilyn Monroe.

DiMaggio, unlike all the other men who wanted to meet the starlet, knew that he actually had a chance. For as little as he liked the trappings of fame, he had grown accustomed to it and sometimes enjoyed the perks, which included meeting some of the world's most beautiful women.

Stars Collide

A blind date between the two was arranged. It was a double date for which Monroe arrived two hours late. DiMaggio wasn't put off or angry because of her lateness. He waited patiently, and when she finally did arrive, something clicked.

Then a retired baseball legend, DiMaggio courted and eventually married Marilyn Monroe, who would soon become one of the most famous actresses of all time.

From that night on, they saw as much of each other as possible until DiMaggio had to return to New York where he was to begin his second career as a Yankee broadcaster. He left Los Angeles reluctantly. He didn't want to leave Monroe, and he could hardly face the fact that he would be returning to Yankee Stadium as an outsider and—even worse—as a member of the press, with whom he'd always had an uneasy relationship.

When Monroe wrapped up work on a film that she had been working on, she flew out to New York to be with DiMaggio. The famous couple literally lit up the city. Flashlights popped wherever they went, and before long they were a national news item. Soon, the American public was as much in love with the idea of Joe and Marilyn as the two were with each other.

When Monroe returned to Los Angeles to work, DiMaggio called her each night without fail. At the end of the season (with the Yanks winning another World Series in Game 7, after Mantle hit a home run), he headed west to be with her.

As happy as the two may have seemed as a couple, behind the scenes they were already butting heads. It was one thing for DiMaggio to admire Monroe's good looks, but as the couple grew closer, it became increasingly difficult for him to deal with the pull she had on men in general.

Raised by a conservative Catholic woman who barely left the house, DiMaggio, who never relished his fame in the first place, wanted more often than not to spend quiet nights at home. When they did go out, he was often enraged by the low-cut, sexy dresses she chose to wear.

Their age difference was also an issue. DiMaggio's glory days were behind him, but at twenty-five, Monroe's career was just beginning. It didn't help that the press scrutinized their every move, in many cases misreading or over-blowing interactions between them.

Despite all the challenges, however, the two stuck it out. At the end of the day, her sparkling personality cheered DiMaggio, and his stoic dependability grounded her and made her feel loved and protected. For all their differences, they shared not only an inexplicable chemistry but also an understanding of the pain of crushing fame.

The couple frequently spent time in San Francisco in the home DiMaggio had bought for his parents after his second year in the majors. Though most of his siblings had left home, one of his sisters was still there, as well as frequently visiting grandchildren, cousins, and other family members. For Monroe, who spent her childhood in foster homes, the atmosphere felt perfect.

DiMaggio's experience in negotiating for a decent contract also came in handy when Monroe began to battle over money issues with the movie studio to which she was signed. As he did almost twenty years previous, he advised Monroe to stand her ground and not give into the demands of the studio president, who was threatening to destroy her career.

Wedding Bells Ring

On January 14, 1954, nearly two years after they met, DiMaggio and Monroe married in a civil ceremony in San Francisco. The unannounced wedding was over in minutes, but someone tipped off the press, and when the newlyweds left City Hall, they were met by crowds of reporters, photographers, and fans.

As Monroe's fame grew and the demand for her as an actress increased, the couple began to spend more time apart, and when they were together, they often argued. Like his marriage to Dorothy, his marriage to Marilyn

DiMaggio and Monroe embrace at their wedding in San Francisco in January 1954.

turned into a heartbreaking cycle of breakups and reconciliations.

After one particularly intense fight, in which it was rumored that DiMaggio shoved Monroe, she had had enough. She filed for divorce just nine months after they had married. The news filled the papers for days.

Perhaps DiMaggio's only consolation in the months following the divorce was his induction into baseball's Hall of Fame in 1955. It didn't do much to cheer him up, though, since he felt that he should have received the induction two years earlier when he had first become eligible.

Divorced or not, DiMaggio was still very much in love with Monroe, and though she did her best to move on with her life, he persisted. Eventually, she gave in and the couple continued to see each other on and off until she married celebrated playwright Arthur Miller on June 29, 1956.

Even during her marriage to Miller, Monroe and DiMaggio continued to communicate. By then, Monroe was struggling with addictions to alcohol and other drugs. Soon after it was announced that another divorce was imminent, she suffered a mental breakdown and was checked into a psychiatric hospital.

After three days, the doctors, who refused to release her, allowed her one telephone call. She immediately contacted DiMaggio, who wasted no time in traveling from Florida, where he was helping to coach the Yankees, to California to aid in her release. Throughout the rest of her life, DiMaggio would maintain a role as her faithful friend and guardian, coming to her rescue and taking care of her whenever her life spun out of control.

In 1962, at the age of thirty-six, Monroe died of a drug overdose. DiMaggio not only identified her body but quickly took over the funeral arrangements. Convinced that Hollywood had killed her, he allowed only a small, select group to attend the funeral, banning several of her more famous friends.

Some say that until the day he died, DiMaggio carried a torch for Marilyn Monroe. For many years after she passed away, as she had once requested, he paid for the bi-weekly delivery of a dozen red roses to her gravesite.

Like a true gentleman, DiMaggio rarely spoke a word about her or their relationship to anyone. Reporters knew better than even to attempt to broach the subject. Any questions related to Monroe were sure to be met by an icy stare and possibly a declaration that the interview was officially finished.

Eight years after their marriage, a grief-stricken DiMaggio enters the Westwood Village Mortuary to take care of Marilyn's funeral arrangements. Stoic as ever, DiMaggio remained quiet about their relationship for the rest of his life.

Throughout the rest of his life, DiMaggio would receive offers from book and magazine editors to go on the record about Marilyn. In the late 1980s, he was offered $2 million to write an autobiography, which would include information about his relationship with the movie starlet. Although nobody appreciated a good paycheck more than DiMaggio, he flatly rejected the offer.

"Where Have You Gone, Joe DiMaggio?"

Had Joe DiMaggio been any other player, perhaps the public would have allowed him to fade quietly into obscurity after Monroe's death. The public, however, simply couldn't forget him.

One of his biggest fans included Charlie Finley, owner of the Oakland Athletics. In 1967, Finley offered DiMaggio a coaching position, which he accepted. Though he stayed on for just two years, it was rumored that DiMaggio was offered managerial positions with other major league teams, but he simply wasn't interested.

It was during the same period that the well-known songwriting duo Simon and Garfunkel penned the song "Mrs. Robinson," which included the line "Where have you gone, Joe DiMaggio? A nation turns its lonely eyes to you."

DiMaggio giving orders as executive vice president and coach of the Oakland Athletics in 1968.

The song rose to number one on the pop charts and not only reintroduced the baseball great to a whole new generation but further established his legendary staying power. In *I Remember Joe DiMaggio*, Yankee shortstop Derek Jeter is quoted as saying, "Joe DiMaggio has a song. That brings it to another level."

In a *New York Times* essay penned after DiMaggio's death by the song's author, Paul Simon, he recalls meeting up with DiMaggio years after the song was popular. Simon had heard that DiMaggio was upset with the song and had considered a lawsuit. Not knowing what type of reception he would get, he walked over to DiMaggio's table with trepidation and introduced himself.

Simon was greeted graciously and asked to join the table. It didn't take long for the topic of the song to come up, and DiMaggio asked Simon to explain why he had written the lyric. Simon explained in the same *New York Times* essay that he didn't mean the lines literally, but that he "thought of [DiMaggio] as an American hero and that genuine heroes were in short supply."

Public Endorsements

Younger generations that had only heard about DiMaggio got a chance to see him in the 1970s, when he signed on with both the Bowery Bank and Mr. Coffee as a spokesman. Both campaigns were successful, in particular his role as spokesman for Bowery Bank, for whom he appeared on televised ads for more than ten years.

Despite all his achievements, or perhaps because of them, DiMaggio's personal relationships with family were often difficult, starting with his own son, with whom he was never close. When his son was young, their opportunities to be involved were hurt by the dissolution of his marriage to Dorothy and his career, which kept him on the road over the years.

Although Joe Jr. appeared to be heading in the right direction as a young adult—he attended Yale University and did a short stint in the marines—in reality he felt crushed by his father's fame. In his late twenties, he married a single mother with two small daughters, though the union didn't last. By then, Joe Jr. was already struggling with a drug addiction that would further estrange him from his father.

To DiMaggio's credit, he never turned his back on his son, and he did develop a close relationship with his son's two stepdaughters, Paula and Kathie, whom he treasured as if they were his own grandchildren.

DiMaggio lived most of his latter years in Florida, though he continued to make frequent visits to New York City. In 1998, he was invited to a dinner organized by *Time* magazine, which was celebrating its 75th anniversary as well as honoring all the people who had been featured on its cover.

According to *The Hero's Life*, several individuals stood up to speak and give toasts to great historic figures. When Bill Clinton spoke, he toasted Franklin Roosevelt; Toni Morrison spoke about Martin Luther King Jr. When actor Kevin Costner stood to speak, he toasted Joe DiMaggio. "To this day, when I hear the name Joe DiMaggio, it is so much more than a man's name. It reminds me to play whatever game I'm in with more grace, pride, and dignity." He added,

DiMaggio talks with lawyer F. Lee Bailey at Radio City Music Hall during *Time* magazine's 75th anniversary celebration.

"When I step into the yard to play catch with my son—whose name is Joe—I think about the Joe we are honoring tonight. I wish that both of us could go to the ballpark and see him play. Because men like Joe DiMaggio are not just of their own time. They are men for the ages."

When he finished, a banquet hall full of some of the world's most accomplished people stood and gave him the longest ovation that night. At age 83, DiMaggio wasn't too old to graciously receive one more loud round of applause from his adoring fans.

His Final Appearance

Later that year, in September, DiMaggio would make what would be his last public appearance at Yankee Stadium for "Joe DiMaggio Day." He appeared to be in poor heath, and when he returned to Florida, he checked into the hospital with breathing difficulties. A cancerous tumor was removed from his left lung, and after a difficult convalescence, he was released from the hospital in January 1999.

While recovering, he consented to seeing very few visitors, including his brother Dom (the rest of his immediate family had all passed away), his two granddaughters, and Yankee owner George Steinbrenner. The recovery never came. Late in the night on March 8, 1999, at age 84, DiMaggio's tired body could no longer continue. He died quietly, surrounded by a handful of friends and family.

His funeral was held three days later in San Francisco. There were only 30 people

Outside of DiMaggio's funeral, devoted New York Yankees fans hold up a sign in his honor.

present, and most of them were DiMaggio's cousins. Joe's brother Dom spoke, and his son, Joe Jr., acted as one of the pallbearers. Within six months, DiMaggio's troubled son would die from a drug overdose.

A month after DiMaggio's death, the Yankees honored the legend by placing a monument to him in Yankee Stadium. Monuments to other Yankee greats, including Lou Gehrig, Babe Ruth, and Mickey Mantle, appeared beside it. As long as Yankee Stadium stands, and surely even after, DiMaggio's place in history as one of the great ones would be set in stone.

Legacy

In 1969, at the All-Star Game banquet, Babe Ruth was voted the Greatest All Time Player, and DiMaggio was chosen as the game's Greatest Living Player. It would be interesting to see how that same vote would turn out if the poll were taken today.

If anything, in the years since DiMaggio retired, his legacy has grown. After all, while Ruth's home-run record has been surpassed, no

Batting

Year	Tm	Lg	G	AB	R	H	2B	3B	HR	RBI	BA
1936	NYY	AL	138	637	132	206	44	15	29	125	.323
1937	NYY	AL	151	621	151	215	35	15	46	167	.346
1938	NYY	AL	145	599	129	194	32	13	32	140	.324
1939	NYY	AL	120	462	108	176	32	6	30	126	.381
1940	NYY	AL	132	508	93	179	28	9	31	133	.352
1941	NYY	AL	139	541	122	193	43	11	30	125	.357
1942	NYY	AL	154	610	123	186	29	13	21	114	.305
1946	NYY	AL	132	503	81	146	20	8	25	95	.290
1947	NYY	AL	141	534	97	168	31	10	20	97	.315
1948	NYY	AL	153	594	110	190	26	11	39	155	.320
1949	NYY	AL	76	272	58	94	14	6	14	67	.346
1950	NYY	AL	139	525	114	158	33	10	32	122	.301
1951	NYY	AL	116	415	72	109	22	4	12	71	.263
13 Seasons			1,736	6,821	1,390	2,214	389	131	361	1,537	.325

player in the league has come close to DiMaggio's hitting streak of 56 games.

Additionally, DiMaggio, who was chosen for the All-Star Team every year of his career and won the MVP award three times, has been to the World Series more than any player in history. Ten times he led his team to the World Series and played in every game. Nine out of those ten times, he came home with a new ring for his finger.

Of course, with DiMaggio, it was always so much more than a numbers game. Beyond just his play, he was both highly focused and extremely

JOSEPH PAUL DI MAGGIO
NEW YORK A.L. 1936 TO 1951

HIT SAFELY IN 56 CONSECUTIVE GAMES
FOR MAJOR LEAGUE RECORD 1941. HIT 2
HOME-RUNS IN ONE INNING 1936. HIT 3
HOME-RUNS IN ONE GAME (3 TIMES). HOLDS
NUMEROUS BATTING RECORDS. PLAYED IN
10 WORLD SERIES (51 GAMES) AND 11 ALL
STAR GAMES. MOST VALUABLE PL
A.L. 1939, 1941, 1947.

In Cooperstown, New York, DiMaggio's plaque rests in the National Baseball Hall of Fame.

Hitting Streaks

The longest hitting streak by a left-handed batter is 44 games by Willie Keeler in 1897. The longest streak by a right-handed batter is 56 games by Joe DiMaggio. Pete Rose's 44-game streak in 1978 is the longest ever by a switch-hitter.

Player	Year	Team	Lg	G	Player	Year	Team	Lg	G
Joe DiMaggio	1941	NY	A	56	Ed Delahanty	1899	Phi	N	31
Willie Keeler	1897	Bal	N	44	Nap Lajoie	1906	Cle	A	31
Pete Rose	1978	Cin	N	44	Sam Rice	1924	Was	A	31
Bill Dahlen	1894	Chi	N	42	Willie Davis	1969	LA	N	31
George Sisler	1922	Stl	A	41	Rico Carty	1970	Atl	N	31
Ty Cobb	1911	Det	A	40	Ken Landreaux	1980	Min	A	31
Paul Molitor	1987	Mil	A	39	Vladimir Guerrero	1999	Mon	N	31
Tommy Holmes	1945	Bos	N	37	Cal McVey	1876	Chi	N	30
Billy Hamilton	1894	Phi	N	36	Elmer Smith	1898	Cin	N	30
Fred Clarke	1895	Lou	N	35	Tris Speaker	1912	Bos	A	30
Ty Cobb	1917	Det	A	35	Goose Goslin	1934	Det	A	30
George Sisler	1925	Stl	A	34	Stan Musial	1950	Stl	N	30
George McQuinn	1938	Stl	A	34	Ron LeFlore	1976	Det	A	30
Dom DiMaggio	1949	Bos	A	34	George Brett	1980	KC	A	30
Benito Santiago	1987	SD	N	34	Jerome Walton	1989	Chi	N	30
George Davis	1893	NY	N	33	Nomar Garciaparra	1997	Bos	A	30
Hal Chase	1907	NY	A	33	Sandy Alomar, Jr.	1997	Cle	A	30
Rogers Hornsby	1922	Stl	N	33	Eric Davis	1998	Bal	A	30
Heinie Manush	1933	Was	A	33	Luis Gonzalez	1999	Ari	N	30

determined. His gift for the game combined with his stoic personality may have sometimes intimidated his teammates, but it also never failed to push them to work a little harder. Even today, and for generations to come, Joltin' Joe is sure to continue to amaze and inspire.

JOE DIMAGGIO *TIMELINE*

	Nov. 25 1914	Joe DiMaggio is born in Collinsville, California.
	1931	DiMaggio signs up with the Jolly Nights, a local club team.
	1932	Recruited by the San Francisco Seals, DiMaggio plays for a minor league team.
	1933	DiMaggio negotiates a contract to play his first full season in the minors.
	1936	Finally making his major league debut, DiMaggio becomes a New York Yankee.
	Oct. 1936	DiMaggio helps to lead the team to his first World Series.
	1938	After a season batting .380, he is voted MVP.
	1939	DiMaggio marries his fiancée, Dorothy Arnold.
	July 17 1941	"The Streak" ends at 56 games against the Cleveland Indians.
	Oct. 23 1941	Dorothy Arnold gives birth to DiMaggio's first and only child, Joe Jr.
	1943	Dorothy Arnold files for divorce.
	1944	DiMaggio announces that he will enlist with the U.S. Air Force.
	1945	DiMaggio is granted a medical discharge from the air force.

⚾	**1947**	DiMaggio undergoes surgery to remove bone spurs. Later in the season, he is awarded the MVP award.
⚾	**1949**	DiMaggio signs for $100,000, making him the highest-paid player in the major leagues.
⚾	**1950**	In an 8–2 victory over the Cleveland Indians, DiMaggio gets his 2000th career hit.
⚾	**Dec. 1951**	DiMaggio announces his retirement from baseball.
⚾	**April 1952**	"Joltin' Joe" begins a second career as a Yankee broadcaster, performing postgame interviews with players.
⚾	**Jan. 14 1954**	In a second marriage for both, DiMaggio and Monroe wed in San Francisco, California.
⚾	**Oct. 1954**	After a rocky nine months, Monroe files for divorce.
⚾	**1955**	DiMaggio is inducted into baseball's Hall of Fame.
⚾	**1967**	Charlie Finley, owner of the Oakland Athletics, hires DiMaggio for a coaching position.
⚾	**1972**	DiMaggio is hired as a spokesman for the Bowery Bank and, later, Mr. Coffee.
⚾	**1998**	DiMaggio appears in Yankee Stadium for "Joe DiMaggio Day."
⚾	**Oct. 1998**	DiMaggio has surgery to remove a cancerous tumor in his left lung.
⚾	**March 8, 1999**	DiMaggio dies at the age of 84.

Glossary

base hit   A hit that results in a batter reaching first, second, or third base, or home plate safely on a fair ball.

batting average   The number of hits divided by the number of at bats. A .300 batting average (180 hits in 600 at bats) is a standard goal.

exhibition game   A game that doesn't count in regular-season standings or records; usually played during spring training.

fly ball   A batted ball hit high, giving the fielder enough time to make an easy catch.

Great Depression   The period of economic hardship and widespread unemployment during the 1930s.

MVP   Most valuable player.

on deck   Waiting for a turn at bat after the current batter.

rookie   A first-year player.

runs batted in (RBIs)   Runs that a batter drives home via a hit, sacrifice bunt or fly, walk, fielder's choice, or error.

scout   A person who seeks out talented young players to be signed by major league teams.

strike out   When a batter swings and misses three pitches, receives three pitches within the strike zone without swinging, or a combination of the two. The batter is then declared out. Foul balls are counted as strikes, except for the third strike, which either must be a swing-and-a-miss or looking.

switch hitter   A batter who can hit either right-handed or left-handed.

World Series   The championship series matching the winners of the American League and the National League. The series is preceded by Divisional and League Championship series in each league. The World Series is a best-of-seven affair that takes place in October and has been held annually since 1903 (except in 1904 and 1994).

For More Information

Major League Baseball
75 9th Avenue
New York, NY 10011
(646) 486-0006
Web site: http://www.majorleaguebaseball.com

National Baseball Hall of Fame and Museum
25 Main Street
P.O. Box 590
Cooperstown, NY 13326
(888) Hall-of-Fame (425-5633)
Web site: http://www.baseballhalloffame.org

Web Sites

Due to the changing nature of Internet links, the Rosen Publishing Group, Inc., has developed an online list of Web sites related to the subject of this book. This site is updated regularly. Please use this link to access the list:

http://www.rosenlinks.com/bhf/jdim/

For Further Reading

Cataneo, David. *I Remember Joe DiMaggio: Personal Memories of the Yankee Clipper by the People Who Knew Him Best* (I Remember Series). Nashville, TN: Cumberland House, 2001.

Cramer, Richard Ben. *Joe DiMaggio: The Hero's Life*. New York: Touchstone Books, 2001.

DiMaggio, Joe. *Baseball for Everyone*. New York: McGraw Hill, 2002.

Seidel, Michael. *Streak: Joe DiMaggio and the Summer of '41*. Lincoln, NE: University of Nebraska Press, 2002.

Stout, Glenn. *DiMaggio: An Illustrated Life*. New York: Walker & Co., 1995.

Testa, Maria. *Becoming Joe DiMaggio*. Cambridge, MA: Candlewick Press, 2002.

Bibliography

Cataneo, David. *I Remember Joe DiMaggio: Personal Memories of the Yankee Clipper by the People Who Knew Him Best* (I Remember Series). Nashville, TN: Cumberland House, 2001.

Cramer, Richard Ben. *Joe DiMaggio: The Hero's Life*. New York: Touchstone Books, 2001.

De Gregorio, George. *Joe DiMaggio: An Informal Biography*. Briarcliff Manor, NY: Stein and Day, 1981.

DiMaggio, Joe. *Baseball for Everyone*. New York: McGraw Hill College Division, 2002.

Durso, Joseph. *DiMaggio: The Last American Knight*. New York: Little, Brown & Company, 1995.

Gilliam, Richard. *Joltin' Joe DiMaggio*. New York: Carol & Graf Publishers, 1999.

Johnson, Dick. *DiMaggio: An Illustrated Life*. New York: Walker & Co., 1995.

Kahn, Roger. *Joe & Marilyn*. New York: Avon Books, 1986.

Index

About the Author

Lois Sakany is a writer and a lifelong Bronx Bombers fan who lives in Brooklyn, New York. This is her second book for young readers.

Photo Credits

Cover, pp. 12, 23, 26, 28, 30, 36, 39, 42–43, 55, 56, 68, 72, 82, 86 © Bettmann/Corbis; p. 4 © Hy Peskin/TimePix; p. 8 © Carl Mydans/TimePix; pp. 10, 17, 20, 47, 48, 60, 63, 65, 75, 78, 89, 91, 95, 100 © AP/Wide World Photos; p. 97 © AFP/Corbis.

Editor

Joann Jovinelly

Series Design and Layout

Geri Giordano